Merry Christmas,
HELLO KITTY®

Abrams Books for Young Readers
New York

Hello Kitty loves everything about Christmas!

Every year Hello Kitty spends time with her family and friends, enjoying all of the wonderful things about the season.

When it snows, Hello Kitty and Mimmy go sledding. It's so much fun to ride down the hill!

With the help of her friends, Hello Kitty builds a snowman and gives him a hat, scarf, and mittens.

Next, the friends go caroling to spread holiday cheer.

They sing Christmas songs to all the neighbors.
They are a big hit!

When it's time to come in from the cold,
Mama makes hot chocolate.

They sit down at the table and warm up.
Brr—it's cold outside!

Hello Kitty likes to help Mama bake Christmas cookies.
She gets out the ingredients and mixes the batter.

The most fun part is decorating the cookies with sprinkles after they've cooled.

Next, Hello Kitty and Mimmy decorate the house with garlands, bows, and wreaths.

They also add some mistletoe!

Hello Kitty and Mimmy hang their stockings above the fireplace.
They make sure to hang stockings for Mama and Papa.

After they hang their stockings, Hello Kitty and Mimmy decorate the tree with ornaments. They put all their presents for each other under the tree to open on Christmas morning.

Papa adds the twinkling star to the top.

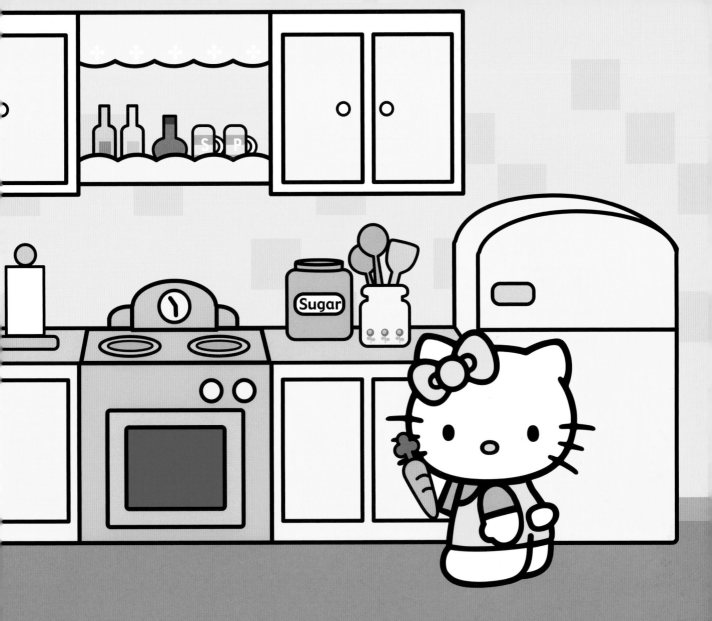

On Christmas Eve, Hello Kitty and Mimmy leave cookies and milk for Santa and carrots for the reindeer.

As they climb into bed, Hello Kitty and Mimmy imagine Santa and his reindeer flying through the night to deliver presents. What will he bring this year?

Christmas morning is finally here, and Hello Kitty has so many wonderful presents from Santa.

The best present is being able to enjoy all the things about the season with her family and friends. Merry Christmas, Hello Kitty!

ISBN: 978-1-4197-1376-7

Published in 2014 by Abrams Books for Young Readers, an imprint of ABRAMS.
Previously published by Abrams in 2003. All rights reserved. No portion of this
book may be reproduced, stored in a retrieval system, or transmitted in any
form or by any means, mechanical, electronic, photocopying, recording, or
otherwise, without written permission from the publisher.

Printed and bound in China
10 9 8 7 6 5 4 3 2 1

Abrams Books for Young Readers are available at special discounts when
purchased in quantity for premiums and promotions as well as fundraising
or educational use. Special editions can also be created to specification. For
details, contact specialsales@abramsbooks.com or the address below.

THE ART OF BOOKS SINCE 1949
115 West 18th Street
New York, NY 10011
www.abramsbooks.com